When I Was a Baby

First published 2007
Evans Brothers Limited
2A Portman Mansions
Chiltern Street
London W1U 6NR

British Library Cataloguing in Publication Data

Goodey, Madeleine
    When I was a baby. - (Twisters)
    1. Newborn infants - Pictorial works - Juvenile fiction
    2. Children's stories - Pictorial works
    I. Title
    823.9'2[J]

ISBN-10: 0 237 53338 3 (hb)
ISBN-13: 978 0 237 53338 0 (hb)

ISBN-10: 0 237 53334 0 (pb)
ISBN-13: 978 0 237 53334 2 (pb)

Printed in China

Series Editor: Nick Turpin
Design: Robert Walster
Production: Jenny Mulvanny

When I Was a Baby

Madeline Goodey
and Amy Brown

Evans

When I was a baby I...

...slept in a cot...

…and drank from a bottle.

Not now!

I sucked my thumb…

13

...and dribbled...

...and cried.

Not now!

I threw my toys…

...and wet my nappy.

Not now!

When I was a baby…

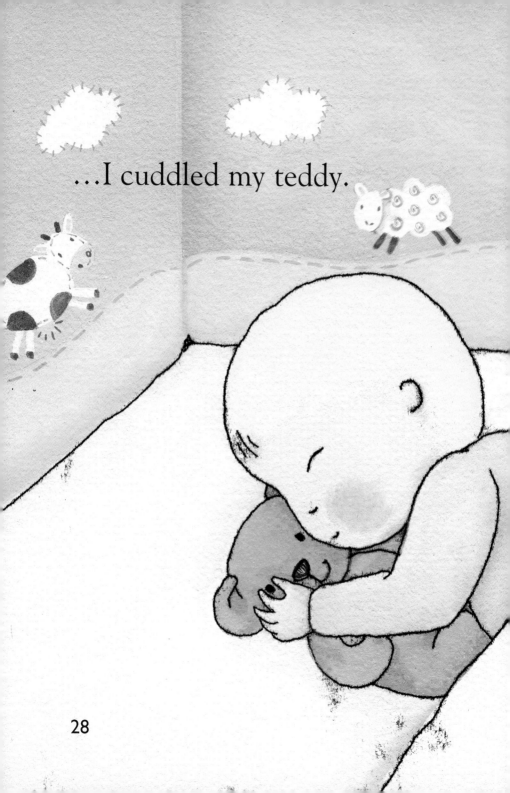

...I cuddled my teddy.

28

And I still do!

Why not try reading another Twisters book?